D0614413

Go on all of Zac's missions in

#1 POISON ISLAND

#2 DEEP WATERS

#3 MIND GAMES

#4 FROZEN FEAR

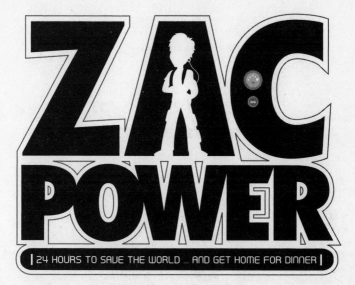

24 HOURS TO SAVE THE WORLD ... AND GET HOME FOR DINNER

MIND GAMES

BY H. I. LARRY

ILLUSTRATIONS BY ASH OSWALD

SQUARE
FISH

FEIWEL AND FRIENDS
New York

With special thanks to the spies of
Years 2 and 3 (2005) of the St. Michael's unit of GIB
for their top secret mission support.

SQUARE
FISH

An Imprint of Macmillan
175 Fifth Avenue
New York, NY 10010
mackids.com

ZAC POWER: MIND GAMES. Text copyright © 2006 by H. I. Larry.
Illustration and design copyright © 2006 by Hardie Grant Egmont.
All rights reserved. Printed in the United States of America by
R. R. Donnelley & Sons Company, Harrisonburg, Virginia.

Square Fish and the Square Fish logo are trademarks of Macmillan and
are used by Feiwel and Friends under license from Macmillan.

Library of Congress Cataloging-in-Publication Data Available
ISBN 978-0-312-34657-7

Originally published in Australia by Hardie Grant Egmont.
Illustration and design by Ash Oswald.
First published in the United States by Feiwel and Friends
First Square Fish Edition: April 2013
Square Fish logo designed by Filomena Tuosto

10 9 8 7 6 5

AR: 4.1 / LEXILE: 600L

CHAPTER ONE

One afternoon, Zac Power was shopping for cool new sneakers at the Westbridge Mall.

Zac was a bit of an expert on the subject of being cool. He was 12 years old, and he worked as a spy for the Government Investigation Bureau, or GIB for short.

As he shopped, Zac watched out for people he knew. He didn't want anyone from school to think he cared how he looked. That would be trying too hard.

At Hot Diggity, the hot dog shop, Ann and her best friend Lucy were giggling into their milkshakes. Girls!

His favorite CD shop, Tunez, was full of kids from school. The whole world seemed to be hanging out at Westbridge. But Zac slipped by them all, unnoticed.

Zac headed towards Sports Station. Inside, the music was so loud the walls were shaking. It was rock music, the only kind Zac liked. Sports Station had the best sneakers at Westbridge. Zac's favorites were a pair with green and yellow stripes on the side.

Zac picked them up. Right away, a sales guy bounced over. A plastic nametag on a cord around his neck read, "Davo."

"How're you doing, man?" asked Davo.

"Can I try these? Size . . . uh . . . eight?" Zac said.

"Sure thing. I'll go check in the back."

The sales guy disappeared into the storeroom. Zac waited. He looked at some T-shirts. No sales assistant. He picked up a magazine and checked out the photos of kids skateboarding down stair rails in the latest clothes. Still no Davo.

What is he doing back there?

Suddenly, Davo reappeared, a shoebox in his hand and a weird look on his face.

"We didn't have size eight in the green and yellow. But why don't you try these?"

He opened the box. Inside, Zac saw a pair of the ugliest sneakers *ever*. They were grey, the color of belly button lint. The soles were twice as thick as ordinary sneakers. They were covered in wires and flashing lights.

"Nah, that's OK, thanks," said Zac, heading for the door.

"Come on! They're limited edition. I guarantee no one else'll have a pair like them."

Zac rolled his eyes. "No one would want to!"

Davo pulled the grey sneakers out of the box.

"Just try 'em."

Heaving a big sigh, Zac grabbed the shoes and pulled them on. They felt even worse than they looked!

As soon as his feet were inside, clamps grabbed Zac's ankles. He stood up and couldn't help wobbling as he took a step.

Each sneaker must have weighed about 100 pounds.

"What do you think?" asked Davo.

Zac shook his head. "I might wait 'til you get the others in."

"Oh, come on, Zac. Just take them."

Zac? How did this guy know my name?

Davo leaned over to pick up the box. His nametag flipped over and Zac caught a glimpse of the back.

Was it? Yes, it was! The GIB crest!

Davo grabbed Zac by the arm and whispered in his ear, "They're yours, OK? Now get out of here."

Before Zac could stop him, Davo disappeared with Zac's old sneakers. Great!

Now Zac had to walk all the way home in the weird grey sneakers.

He stepped out of Sports Station. Ann and Lucy had finished their milkshakes and gone home. Maybe he was safe. . . .

Then . . .

Kerrr-BOOOOOOM!

There was an earsplitting explosion. A cloud of white smoke. The gross grey sneakers had exploded!

Zac shot up off the ground. He flew through the air, propelled by his exploding sneakers. They had the force of ten rockets. No, make that 100 rockets!

Zac shot past Hot Diggity. Tunez was a blur. He was flying toward a set of elevators.

The metal doors were closed. Yikes! He was going to smash right into them.

At the very last second, the elevator doors opened. And suddenly, Zac was falling. He looked up and saw the elevator stuck high above him. He was falling straight down the elevator shaft.

Round and round, faster and faster he fell in a midair forward roll.

At the bottom of the elevator shaft, Zac landed with a thud on hard, cold concrete. Lucky he had been taught how to land safely during GIB training, or he would have broken a bone for sure.

The elevator doors opened with a ping.

Zac was in an underground parking

garage. Parked nearby was a white van with a satellite dish on top. The door opened and a strong pair of arms dragged Zac into the back.

The door slammed shut and, with a screech of tires, the van took off.

Zac looked down at his feet. The exploding sneakers were completely gone. All that was left was a very holey, smoky pair of socks.

"Hello, Zac," said the strong-armed man, who was driving the van. "I've been expecting you."

CHAPTER TWO

"I'm Agent-in-Training Gorman, GIB Transport Division," said the man. "Hope that wasn't too uncomfortable, Zac," he went on, looking guiltily at Zac's socks. "I've just transferred from Stationery and Supplies, actually. You're my first agent pickup."

Zac remembered his first solo mission. He smiled at Gorman.

It wasn't easy being the new guy.

"Do you know the way to the airport, Zac?" asked Gorman.

"The airport? Why? What's my mission?" said Zac.

Gorman fished around in his pockets. "It's somewhere in here," Gorman muttered to himself.

At last he found what he was looking for. He handed Zac a small metal disc.

Zac loaded the disc into his SpyPad. Every GIB spy had a SpyPad. It looked sort of like an electronic game, but really it was a minicomputer with built-in GPS navigation software, a laser, and a code-breaker, all rolled into one.

CLASSIFIED
MISSION INITIATED 9:00 AM

Unknown hostiles are hacking into the
computer system controlling WorldEye.
WorldEye is GIB's satellite system,
so powerful it can read a newspaper
headline from 500 miles away.
The software is protected by encrypted
passwords and high-level firewalls.
Still, the hackers have managed
to breach every firewall but one.

YOUR MISSION
- Locate hackers.
- Discover why they want to
  hack into WorldEye.
- Prevent breaching of final firewall.

END

FOOTBALL SCORE
>>> OFF

This was bad!

Only one firewall standing between WorldEye and a bunch of criminals!

"What does Leon think?" asked Zac, as the van turned onto the freeway toward the airport.

Leon, Zac's brother, was a Technical Support Officer with GIB. If anyone knew how to handle computer hackers, it was Leon.

"Leon's tracked the hackers to the city of Bladesville," said Gorman.

Zac fought back a proud smile. Sometimes nerdy brothers really did come in handy.

"You wouldn't be smiling if you knew

anything about Bladesville," said Gorman. His eyes widened. "I've heard it's one of the meanest, toughest, dirtiest cities in the whole world."

Zac said nothing. Whatever Bladesville had in store for him, he could deal with it. Couldn't he?

"Oh, yeah," Gorman went on. "Leon reckons it'll take the hackers 24 hours to breach the last firewall."

Only 24 hours? Zac did some quick calculations in his head.

Now he was freaking out!

"Says here the mission started at 9 a.m. today, so that means I've only got until 9 a.m. tomorrow to fly to Bladesville and stop the hackers. And it's"—Zac glanced at his watch—"already 6:51 p.m.!"

Gordon looked guilty for a moment.

"Yeah, sorry about the delay in getting you on the mission, Zac. First time and everything, you see."

Gorman coughed nervously. But Zac could see there wasn't any point getting angry. Gorman was doing the best he could. Was it his fault his best was, um, not really very good?

Gorman opened the van's glove box.

"I nearly forgot these," he said, passing

Zac a pair of wraparound glasses with a computer game controller attached.

"These aren't going to explode too, are they?" Zac asked, thinking of the grey sneakers.

"No, they're virtual reality glasses," said Gorman vaguely.

Zac put the glasses on.

It looked exactly like he was sitting in the cockpit of a fighter jet. Zac grabbed the controller. On screen, it looked like he was touching real fighter jet controls.

"Woah!" said Zac. It was the most realistic virtual reality flight simulator ever.

"Isn't it incredible?" said Gorman. "Ever piloted a fighter jet before?"

Zac hadn't, but he couldn't wait to try. He took hold of the steering yoke. He sped off down the tarmac. He engaged the throttle. Then, with a loud, realistic whoosh of air, he was airborne!

Up Zac flew. He burst through the clouds. He was at 20,000 feet and climbing.

He fiddled with the controls. One was

for speed, one was to turn left and right. *This flying thing doesn't look so hard,* thought Zac.

Then Zac heard a warning siren.

A message flashed on his virtual computer screen.

...STORM ALERT!...

The sky went dark. Purple lightning slashed the sky. The plane shook violently. Zac's fighter had been struck!

The fighter jerked one way, then the other. Zac couldn't get control of the steering. His computer screen flashed again.

...LOSING ALTITUDE!...

The plane took a nosedive.

Helpless, Zac watched the altitude

drop from 20,000 to 10,000 feet in a few seconds. He broke through the clouds. Right below was a mountain range.

He was going to crash!

Zac braced himself for impact. The fighter spun onto its back and slammed into the mountains. It burst into flames.

... GAME OVER! YOU LOSE! ...

Zac ripped off the virtual reality glasses. He was sweating. The plane crash had felt so real!

"All right, Zac?" asked Gorman. "Computer games are so advanced these days. And so addictive! They really play mind games with you."

Ghost white, Zac nodded.

"Well, don't worry. We're at the airport now," said Gorman cheerfully.

The van turned into a secret side entrance. The tarmac was just ahead. And there, waiting for Zac, was a miniature fighter jet.

"Probably should've told you before," said Gorman, absentmindedly. "You're flying yourself to Bladesville. The flight simulator was your training."

Zac said nothing.

A spy always keeps his cool.

"That's OK with you, isn't it, Zac?"

CHAPTER THREE

Zac strode casually across the tarmac towards the mini fighter jet. He raced up the stairs to the cockpit. The controls looked almost the same as the ones in the flight simulator. A radio headset sat on the pilot's seat.

Zac put it on and heard a voice.

"Zac Power, this is Air Traffic Control. The time is 8:09 p.m. Weather conditions are fine. You're cleared for takeoff on runway three."

Zac took hold of the yoke. He engaged the throttle and the engine growled.

The fighter jet taxied across the tarmac. Zac angled the yoke upwards and pushed harder on the throttle. The jet gathered speed. Then, with a loud thump as the wheels folded up, Zac was in the air.

But this time, it was for real!

Steadily, Zac climbed. He pierced the clouds. The sun was out and there was no wind. Perfect flying conditions!

Zac tipped the yoke forward. The plane dipped down. He pulled the yoke up again. The plane shot upward. He pulled the yoke sharp right. The jet flipped over onto its side!

Cool! Zac tried the left-hand side. He shot into a wicked loop-the-loop.

Maybe this wasn't getting him to Bladesville as fast as possible. But it was *so* worth it!

A voice crackled in Zac's radio headset. "Come in, Zac Power."

"Power here," said Zac, as confidently as he could.

"Weather conditions in your airspace have declined," said Air Traffic Control. "A freak electrical storm's heading your way."

Zac looked around. The brilliant sunshine had gone. Heavy black clouds were everywhere.

The fighter started to rattle and bump. Turbulence!

"Suggest emergency landing," said Air Traffic Control.

Zac looked at his watch.

If Zac landed now, it'd take him forever to get to Bladesville and find those hackers. Freak storm or not, Zac was going to have to keep flying.

"Request permission to continue on to Bladesville," said Zac.

There was silence from Air Traffic Control. The fighter roared into a really rough air pocket. The entire cockpit shook. For a second, radio communication dropped out.

The radio came back on. "Permission granted. Proceed at your own risk."

Grimly, Zac flew on. Wind rattled the windshield. The plane lifted and dropped in the wind.

It was worse than an amusement park ride.

The fighter was equipped with rocket-assisted ejector seats. Zac checked where the lever was, just in case. Beside the lever, Zac noticed a button labeled "Vertical Supersonic."

Zac took a deep breath. Could this button possibly do what he hoped? If it climbed at supersonic speed, there was a chance Zac could make it above the storm and out of danger.

Just then, the cockpit lit up as lightning crackled across the sky. These were the conditions that made Zac crash the simulator!

Without thinking, Zac slammed his

hand down on the VERTICAL SUPERSONIC button. Immediately, the fighter jet responded. The nose rose steeply until the plane was speeding straight up.

Then . . .

BOOOOOOM!

A sonic boom!

Zac had broken the speed of sound. He'd gone supersonic!

He streaked upward, leaving the storm behind him. His hands shook. Going vertical supersonic had been as scary as it was awesome.

CHAPTER ... FOUR

Zac jammed on the breaks. He'd been flying so fast he'd hardly noticed he was almost in Bladesville.

Now he had to figure out how and where to land. He took a closer look at the instruments and dials flashing on the dashboard. He noticed a button labeled "Engage Stealth Shield."

Zac hit the button.

Instantly, his mini fighter jet vanished from his radar screen. The stealth shield had turned him invisible!

Zac looked up the location of the Bladesville airport. It was 50 miles out of town. He checked the time.

It was already 11:34 p.m.!

Then Zac had an idea.

If his mini fighter jet was invisible, he could land wherever he wanted!

With that decided, Zac flew down-ward. Skyscrapers stuck up everywhere. The streets were choked with cars and people.

The tallest skyscraper had a huge logo on the side. MindLab. They were some kind of game company. The top of the MindLab building was going to make the perfect landing strip for an invisible mini fighter jet.

Coming in to land, Zac couldn't help switching on the PA system, even though he was alone. This piloting stuff was pretty fun.

"Ladies and gentlemen, this is Captain Zac Power speaking."

His landing was perfect. Not a single bump. Maybe, in another life, Zac could have been a pilot. But he had to shut those thoughts out. He was a spy. He always would be. Zac allowed himself the smallest of sighs.

Zac popped open the invisible cockpit door. He stuck his head out and looked around the top of the MindLab building. A beefy security guard was standing near the only staircase down from the roof into the building.

As usual, Zac had his rappeling gear in his backpack. He'd get down the quick way. Over the side of the building.

All 200 stories!

Around floor 103, Zac's SpyPad beeped. He fished around in his pocket awkwardly—rappeling a hundred floors above a busy street wasn't the perfect time to be checking messages.

It was a cryptic message from GIB Mission Control.

MESSAGE RECEIVED
12:49 AM

Go to
Electric Eel Workshop
Shop 13,
Dank Alley,
Bladesville.
Your contact is Mrs. X.

GPS NAVIGATION
>>> ON

Zac made it down to the street and looked around. He'd never seen such a strange place. It was the middle of the night, but it was still burning hot. Stalls selling food and fake electronic games were everywhere. Music blasted. A monorail snaked overhead.

According to his SpyPad's GPS, Dank Alley was not far.

He zigzagged down alleys smelling of fish heads and garbage. Finally, he found Dank Alley. Shop 13 was at the end, nearly hidden by steam rising up from a gutter.

A sign on the grimy door read, "We're closed, so go away."

Zac knocked anyway.

"Mrs. X?" he called. "It's Zac Power."

Six or seven deadbolts opened. The door swung aside a crack. In the dim light, Zac saw a woman about his own height. Her face was wrinkled, her hair white. A tattoo of an eel twisted up her arm. She looked 120 years old!

"Come," she said in a funny accent. With

a crooked old finger, she directed Zac to the back of the shop. There stood something covered with a dusty old sheet. Whatever it was, Zac couldn't imagine needing it for his mission.

Mrs. X pulled off the sheet. Underneath, was a brand-new hover scooter. There were millions just like it roaring down the streets of Bladesville. Only those were dented and rusty. This one gleamed silver.

"One important addition," said Mrs. X. She pointed at a lever under the handlebar. "Pull up, you fly. Pull down, you sing karaoke."

"This is a karaoke hover scooter?" said Zac, disbelieving. Mrs. X nodded.

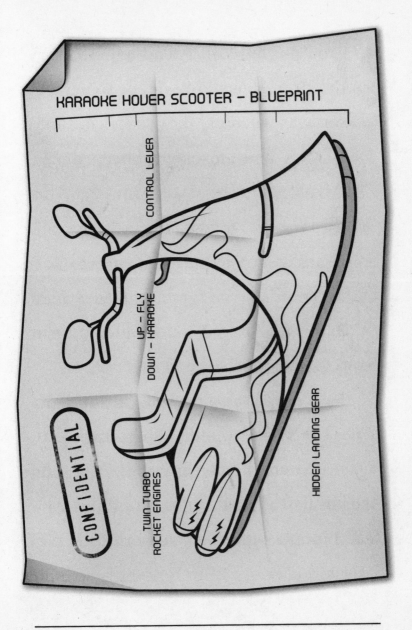

"You go. Tell GIB I send big bill, very soon." Mrs. X started to cackle to herself.

Zac was wheeling the scooter out into Dank Alley when his SpyPad beeped.

"You have one new voice message," the screen flashed.

Zac put the SpyPad to his ear.

"Hello, Zac. Welcome to Bladesville," said a boy's voice—it sounded like a teen-ager.

Could this be one of the hackers? wondered Zac. The voice sounded so young. Then again, Zac and Leon were way better with technical stuff than their mom and dad. Zac's mom couldn't even work the DVD player!

The message went on. "We've been tracking you since you took off. Wonderful thing, WorldEye. Anyway, we found your invisible fighter jet. Pretty cocky, landing on the MindLab building. If you want to live, you better get out of here. Right now."

The hackers were onto him! And, by the sound of things, they'd managed to gain partial control of WorldEye even without breaching the final firewall.

Zac's mission suddenly felt a lot more dangerous.

CHAPTER ...FIVE

Zac crouched in a dark doorway, hidden in shadow. He clutched his SpyPad tight. He was in a foreign city and totally alone. His hands weren't shaking, exactly. But he'd have to admit that the message from the hackers made him edgy.

He punched in the number for GIB Mission Control and asked for Tech Support.

Leon picked up the phone. A friendly voice! Relief flooded through Zac.

"Listen to this message, Leon. I'll patch it through now," said Zac.

Leon listened.

"Nasty," he said. "But don't worry. I'll trace the message. Could lead you straight to the hackers."

Zac waited nervously.

Finally, Leon had something. "The message seems to have come from somewhere within a one-mile radius of your current location," he said.

It was 2:47 a.m. already. Zac had to get a move on!

"Can't you tell me anything else?" asked Zac. "It'll take me weeks to search a square mile in this place."

But Leon couldn't. "They've got a very effective location scrambling device, Zac. These hackers are pretty clued in."

Great! That was all Zac needed to hear!

Zac wasn't sure what to do next, so he replayed the message. This time, he thought he heard something in the background. Music? Yes, it was!

He listened again.

It sounded like "Rotten Lies," a song by one of his favorite bands. But the singing was terrible—the voice was nothing like the lead singer's.

Zac toyed with the handlebars of his new karaoke hover scooter.

Something clicked.

Karaoke! Bladesvillains *loved* karaoke. The hackers must have sent the message from a karaoke bar.

Zac flicked his SpyPad to GPS mode.

Find karaoke bars one mile from here, he typed.

A single name popped up on the screen. The Golden Eardrum Karaoke Cave. Zac jumped on his hover scooter and sped straight there.

It didn't take Zac long to find the Golden Eardrum—it had a bright purple front door and a giant rotating ear on the roof.

He needed to go in and look around without attracting attention. But he knew most of the other customers would be grown-ups. A 12-year-old on his own would really stand out in the crowd.

Then Zac remembered something.

A couple of months ago, Leon had given him a new gadget to road test on a mission. Zac had stuffed it into his backpack and forgotten all about it.

Zac ducked into a nearby alley and pulled out the Protector Projector. The Protector Projector created incredibly realistic 3-D holograms.

All Zac had to do was film himself with the Protector Projector. The Projector would then transmit a hologram of whatever Zac was doing in the footage. It would look absolutely real!

I've got to make it look like I'm doing karaoke, thought Zac. *Then, everyone will be watching my holograph onstage while the real me can look around the Golden Eardrum.*

He looked around the alley carefully. Yes, it seemed deserted. He was going to have to film himself singing in the alley.

Zac set the Protector Projector to record mode. *They like rock music at the Golden Eardrum . . . better do a rock song,* thought Zac.

"Drivin' down the highway, feelin' pretty cool," Zac sang.

How embarrassing! Zac couldn't just stand there, either. To make this perfor-mance look real, he'd have to dance, too. Secretly, he'd always dreamed of being a rock star. Now he had to pretend he really was one!

"No place to go today, not even school," Zac wailed, getting warmed up.

The chorus was pretty cool, actually. Zac played a solo on the air guitar. For once, his dream of becoming a rock star and his spying missions were fitting together perfectly!

Zac hit stop on the Protector Projector and headed for the Golden Eardrum. He was going to track down those hackers if it was the last thing he did. And his hologram was going to put on one awesome show!

CHAPTER SIX

A line snaked out of the Golden Ear-drum. Men in suits shouted and swayed. Women in their best dresses teetered in high-heeled shoes.

None of these people look like hackers, thought Zac. *Actually, they look like an ad for staying at home with a good DVD.*

Just then, the bouncer unclipped the velvet rope blocking the entrance. He waved a couple through, and Zac tagged along behind. He was inside!

The Golden Eardrum was absolutely packed. In a crowd like this, the hackers could be anywhere.

Through a smoky haze, Zac saw a stage at the front of the room. Above that, there was a large screen. Song lyrics appeared on the screen so you could follow along when you were up on stage singing.

Along one wall, he saw what looked like phone booths. They were soundproof karaoke practice booths.

Up on stage, a trio of girls were finishing a horrible, sappy love song.

"Now's my chance!" Zac whispered to

himself. He snuck up to the stage. He hid the Protector Projector under a nearby table and switched it on. A beam of light shot out. Zac aimed it at the stage.

Leon's gadget worked! For there, up on stage, was an absolutely realistic hologram

RECORDED
IMAGE

| >>> RECORD

PROJECTED
HOLOGRAM

CONTROL
PANEL

of Zac singing a rock song at the top of his lungs.

The audience whistled and cheered.

Time for the real Zac to get to work!

Zac scanned the crowd. A group of teenagers stood by the stage, watching the hologram of Zac's awesome performance. *Could they be the hackers?* They looked younger than everyone else in the Golden Eardrum. And it made sense that computer whizzes would be kids.

Just then, Zac's hologram made a strange choking noise.

What? That wasn't in the song!

"Don't wanna be a grown-up, oh no no no," sang the hologram.

Then came the strange choking noise again.

"Oh no no no—"

"Oh no no no—"

The hologram was jammed! It repeated the same line over and over, like a CD skipping. Zac's cover was blown!

A second later, Zac turned back to the teenagers. But they were gone!

Then Zac saw them disappearing into the karaoke practice booth second from the left. He counted seven people going into the booth.

That doesn't seem right, thought Zac. *How could so many kids fit into such a small space?*

Sticking to the shadows, Zac tiptoed over to the booth second from the left. He took a deep breath and threw open the door.

The booth was completely empty!

Looking down, Zac noticed a trapdoor cut into the floor.

The handle was still warm!

Zac heaved open the trapdoor. Down in the gloom, Zac saw a ladder. *Probably leads to the hackers' underground lair,* thought Zac.

Zac had no idea if the hackers would still be down there. But there was only one way to find out. As quietly as he could, Zac snuck down the ladder.

He looked around. With its white walls and bare lightbulbs, the room looked like an ordinary storeroom. The only difference was, it was filled with rows of the latest computers.

If this is the hackers' secret lair, thought Zac, *where are the hackers?*

There was absolutely no one around.

Frustration bubbled up in Zac. He'd been so close! Yet somehow the hackers had slipped away.

Zac took another look around. The hackers had left no trace behind.

No dropped wallet.

No mobile phone.

Not even a single hair.

Except . . .

What on earth was *that thing,* sitting on the floor?

CHAPTER SEVEN

It was the weirdest thing Zac had ever seen. It was shaped like a normal game console, but where the left, right, up, and down buttons should have been, this thing had wires hanging out. Attached to the end of the wires was a shiny metal helmet. It looked like a high-tech version of Zac's mom's colander!

Zac dug out his SpyPad and snapped

a digital photo. Then he e-mailed a copy to Tech Support back at GIB Mission Control. If there was anyone nerdy enough to know what this was, it was Leon.

A few seconds later, Zac's SpyPad rang.

"That's MindLab's latest console, the MindGame 3000!" said Leon, sounding like he was about to burst with excitement.

"What does it do?" asked Zac.

"It's like an ordinary game console, but instead of pressing buttons, you *think* your next move. You can control any computer game just with your mind!"

It sounded cool, but it wasn't going to lead Zac to the hackers.

Leon was carrying on about the Mind-Game 3000. "This is totally amazing! They're not even out on the market yet!" Leon was saying as Zac hung up.

Zac found a door and trailed unhappily out of the basement. He'd never let a mission defeat him before. But this time, with no real leads, he had no idea what to do next. He checked his watch.

Time was running out.

Out in the alley, Zac hopped on his karaoke hover scooter. He was about to roar off when something caught his eye. It was a poster.

GAME CONVENTION
Bladesville Town Hall

TRY OUT THE COOLEST GAMING TECHNOLOGY!

OPEN 24 HOURS

SPONSORED BY MINDLAB

Zac's spy senses zinged. *If the hackers own a game console that isn't even in the stores yet, isn't it possible they're involved in a game convention?*

Zac was going to find out!

He zoomed through the streets of Bladesville toward the town hall. Engaging hover mode, he leapt over trash cans and the occasional dog. In less than ten minutes, Zac was there.

Zac stopped the hover scooter near the front entrance and raced inside. Almost immediately, he felt a hand clamp down on his shoulder.

"Excuse me, sir."

Zac turned and saw a man in a black

suit and dark sunglasses smiling grimly.

"Me?" asked Zac, as innocently as he could. He had to look like an ordinary game-crazy kid, not the super spy he was.

"Congratulations!" said the man, in a strange voice. "You've won a wild card entry into our Grand Game Battle. The best gamers in the world going head-to-head, live on the big screen."

"Er, no thanks. I'd rather just look around the convention," said Zac.

There were hundreds of kids milling around. The hackers were in there some-where, Zac could feel it. He couldn't afford to waste time in some stupid game competition.

"But you've been selected by Mind-Lab, the world's most advanced gaming company. What *normal kid* would pass up a chance like that?" asked the man, his eyes narrowing. "You are a *normal kid*, right?"

"Oh, totally normal," said Zac hastily.

"Well, then. Step this way."

The man slapped a red MindLab baseball cap onto Zac's head and shoved him toward the stage. Two monitors and two game consoles sat waiting for the players. Overhead, a giant screen had been rigged up so everyone at the convention could see who was playing and how they were scoring.

"You know how to play *Flight Night*, right?" said the man. "It's a flight simulator game." Zac shrugged. He had some experience with flight simulators. . . .

More than most of his opponents, it seemed. One by one, Zac clobbered every challenger. It was easy. *Almost too easy,* thought Zac.

Was someone letting him win?

Pretty soon, Zac found himself in the semifinals, leading by one point as the siren sounded. He'd made the grand finale!

Zac checked his watch.

Playing in the grand finale would take up even more time. But even worse, the

8-year-old kid he'd been playing in the semis burst into tears.

"Hey, don't cry," said Zac. "There's always next year."

The kid nodded, not convinced. He pulled his blue MindLab baseball cap down lower to hide his tears. The poor kid was a total *Flight Night* addict, that was obvious.

Zac gazed up at the big screen above their heads. On the screen, all you could really see of the players was the backs of their heads. Maybe . . .

"I've got an idea," said Zac casually. "I'm kind of in a hurry. Could you do me a favor and take my spot in the grand finale?"

The kid's eyes lit up.

"You wear my red cap and I'll wear your blue one. On the big screen, it'll look like it's me playing instead of you," said Zac.

Leaving me free to look for the hackers, Zac added silently to himself.

CHAPTER EIGHT

Zac leapt off the stage. Right away, the crowd swallowed him up. He was safe, at least for the moment.

He thought over everything Leon told him about the mind-controlled game console the hackers left behind.

It was made by MindLab.

If Zac found the MindLab display here at the Game Convention, there was a

good chance the hackers would be some-
where nearby!

It wasn't hard to spot. Over in the cor-
ner, an enormous blinking neon sign read,
"MindLab. Tomorrow's gaming today."

Zac headed over.

MindLab had set up rows of computers
so everyone at the convention could try
their games and equipment.

A thrill rushed through Zac. Every kid
at every computer at the MindLab display
was wearing a high-tech metal helmet!
They were testing the MindLab 3000 console. The hackers must be very close now.

But where? Zac needed to hang back
for a while and watch. But it was already

8:01 a.m. Less than an hour until the fire-wall was breached!

The MindLab display was the most popular stand by far. Kid after kid stepped up to try out the new mind-controlled console. That made sense. *Who wouldn't want to try out something so awesome?*

All the same, Zac couldn't help thinking how rich a company like MindLab must be. *But to keep the money rolling in,* thought Zac, *they need to keep kids addicted to their games.*

Computer games were definitely fun,

but there was also something a little bit creepy about the way they sucked you in.

Suddenly, Zac noticed something strange. When a kid reached a very high score, a man in a black suit and dark sunglasses would appear from nowhere. The man would whisper something in the kid's ear and the two of them would disappear through a door.

As Zac watched, it happened at least three times.

Where are the men taking the gaming champs? And what are they whispering?

Zac dug out his trusty SpyPad. He switched it on and stuck in a pair of headphones. The SpyPad had a high-powered

TURBO DELUXE 2000

SUPERSOUND >>> ON

STUN GUN >>> OFF

multi-directional microphone feature. Zac could hear almost anything, even the softest whisper, from about 150 feet away.

Sneaking closer to the MindLab display, Zac pointed his SpyPad at one of the men in black suits. The man leaned down toward a kid on one of the computers.

"Hey, you're pretty good at that game,"

the man said. The kid hardly looked up.

"My name's Mr. Tait," said the man, sticking out his hand. "How'd you like a job with MindLab? We're hiring champion gamers for an interesting project we're working on. We pay good money."

That got the kid's attention. He nodded, stood up, and walked off with Mr. Tait.

Zac followed along behind, as close as he dared. Mr. Tait and the kid disappeared through a door that said, "Private."

Zac crouched down behind a plant and listened closely. The SpyPad's microphone was so powerful, Zac could hear everything the man said, even through a closed door.

"MindLab is so much more than a gaming company," Mr. Tait was saying. "The technology we invent for games, we also use for much bigger things. Like satellites."

Satellites! Zac's face flushed with excitement. He was about to crack this case, he could feel it.

"At the moment, we're trying to discover how a particularly powerful satellite called WorldEye works," Mr. Tait said. "Since you're so good with the MindLab 3000, we thought you'd be able to help. We use the same controls for our WorldEye project, you see."

So the kid on the other side of the door would be joining a group of kids recruited by MindLab to hack into WorldEye using the MindLab 3000. The hackers Zac followed in the karaoke bar were, too!

The plan was ingenious. Develop the best hacking technology and disguise it as an ordinary game console. Then, recruit the best gamers and pay them lots of money for their silence.

No one would ever suspect kids would be the brains behind a plot as big as hacking into WorldEye.

Just then, the kid on the other side of the door said something to Mr. Tait.

"I thought that satellite belonged to someone else," the kid said. Zac held his breath. *What will Mr. Tait say to that?*

There was a long silence. Then Zac heard the faintest sound. Even with the powerful SpyPad microphone, it was almost too quiet to hear. It was a cross between a sob and a whimper of pain. Zac's blood ran cold.

Zac heard Mr. Tait's cruel voice. "When you work for MindLab, you don't ever ask questions. Now you know why."

Pins and needles prickled Zac's legs. He was going to cramp up if he didn't move soon. He shifted a millimeter to his left. But it was enough. A voice called out.

"Over there! Behind the plant!"

Oh, no! One of the kids from the karaoke bar had spotted Zac.

Before he could run, Zac was surrounded. Zac recognized the man from the front entrance, the one who'd forced him to enter the game competition. He saw all the kids from the karaoke bar. As well as those kids, there were a whole lot of goons he hadn't met yet.

There was no escaping this one!

"I know someone very eager to meet you," said the man from the front entrance in his creepy voice. He grabbed Zac roughly by the arm. "The head of MindLab, Jimmy Shady."

CHAPTER ...NINE

Zac looked around for help. Surely there'd be security guards at the Game Convention? Surely they wouldn't just let a whole bunch of goons march him away in broad daylight?

But then Zac remembered. MindLab was sponsoring the Game Convention. If there were security guards, they worked for MindLab. They'd be no help at all.

Zac needed a plan. But as fast as the goons were dragging him through the hall, there wasn't much time to come up with one. He'd have to think something up on the spot!

"This way," said the man from the front entrance, yanking Zac toward a glass office overlooking the entire convention center.

Magically, the door slid aside. There at a desk was a very short, very ugly man. His thin hair was scraped back against his skull with shiny hair gel. His skin was clammy and pocked like a toad's.

The ugly man stood up and nodded politely. It was like he and Zac were about to sit down to a friendly game of chess.

"Before I kill you," said the ugly man, "let me introduce myself."

Zac knew that a spy must never show fear. Even when his stomach was flip-flopping wildly.

"I'm Jimmy Shady," said the man. "Take a seat. I'll tell you all about my operation."

When he was a kid, Jimmy Shady would've been the last one picked for the baseball team. The one who never got invited to anyone's birthday party. The one who ate lunch all by himself.

Now, Zac could tell Jimmy Shady felt important at last. And he couldn't wait to tell Zac exactly how powerful he really was. In fact, Jimmy Shady was so thrilled with himself, his eyes misted over. He didn't even notice Zac switching on his iPod. That suited Zac just fine.

"Being a GIB spy, you've no doubt figured out I'm recruiting gaming whizzes to help me hack into your precious World-Eye satellite."

Zac nodded. "Why would you want to hack into WorldEye? You're the head of a game company, not an international spy," Zac said. The more Jimmy Shady told him, the better.

"Once I control WorldEye, I'll be able to spy on stupid kids like all the ones out there. I'll be able to find out what they like and don't like. That way, I'll get them all hooked on even more of my super-addictive games!"

"How close are you to controlling WorldEye?" asked Zac.

"One line of computer code away."

Jimmy Shady consulted his notes. "We know the second-to-last line is $H=//t+13$, but we haven't cracked the last line yet. The kids I've recruited today are doing tests right now."

```
>>> H=//t+13
>>> ... ???
```

Zac said nothing.

"Untold riches will be mine! And the funniest part is, I'm using the kids themselves to get even more kids hooked on my games!" Jimmy Shady laughed an evil laugh.

It was all Zac needed to hear. As casually as he could, Zac stretched his arms out. Just the way he'd planned it, something rolled down his sleeve and into his hand.

A stink bomb.

Zac always kept one up his sleeve, just in case. It wasn't anything clever or high tech. But as Zac was learning, sometimes the old-fashioned gadgets were the best.

With all his might, Zac threw the stink bomb at the wall.

It exploded.

Instantly, the room filled with gas.

Jimmy Shady coughed and spluttered. So did his goons. The gas smelled worse than 10,000 dog farts!

Zac sprang to his feet. Before anyone knew what was happening, he'd raced out the door.

He'd managed to secretly record Jimmy Shady admitting his evil plan on the mini video camera in his iPod. Zac had all the evidence he needed to arrest Jimmy and stop the hackers from cracking the final line of computer code.

But how, in a room crawling with Mind-Lab goons, could one 12-year-old arrest the head of MindLab?

CHAPTER ...TEN

Zac tore through the Game Convention
toward the main stage.

With all those monitors and equipment
on the stage, the next part of his plan would
be easy. As quick as lightning, Zac plugged
his iPod into the VIDEO IN jack on the
giant screen.

Zac hit play. Suddenly, Jimmy Shady's
voice boomed through the Bladesville Town

Hall. Everyone stopped what they were doing and looked up. Zac was broadcasting Jimmy Shady's confession for the entire convention to hear.

"Untold riches will be mine! And the

funniest part is, I'm using the kids themselves to get even more kids hooked on my games!" Jimmy Shady said.

All across the hall, kids started talking to each other.

"Hear that?"

"The head of MindLab's been messing with gamers!"

"Let's get him! And the hackers!" Zac heard someone yell.

Like a boiling pot about to overflow, the convention erupted. Kids shouted. Game consoles flew through the air.

It was chaos! The gamers stormed Jimmy Shady's glass office. Within moments, he was captured, handcuffed, and the police were called. Soon, he was driven away in a police car.

Zac's plan had worked perfectly. His mission was complete—thanks to the kids!

Suddenly, Zac heard his SpyPad bleep.

MESSAGE RECEIVED
9:01 AM

Come straight home
once your Bladesville
mission's complete.
Tonight's trash night,
and it's your turn
to take out the garbage.

MESSAGE FROM
AGENT TLC (MOM)

MESSAGE
>>> READ MODE

He'd have to hurry if he was going to make it home in time to take out the trash. But how on earth would he get there? His invisible fighter jet had been stolen by the hackers. There just wasn't time to search for it.

Zac paced up and down outside Jimmy Shady's office. It was empty now, sealed off with black-and-yellow crime scene tape. There was something on the floor, though. Something that looked like . . . yes!

Car keys.

When no one was looking, Zac grabbed the keys. He wasn't going to *steal* Jimmy Shady's car. More like *borrow* it. Just to drive himself to the Bladesville airport so he could get a flight home.

There was always his karaoke hover scooter. But somehow Zac suspected Jimmy Shady would have something much faster, much cooler, he could use.

Zac raced to the parking lot outside the town hall. There were hundreds of cars parked there!

Which one was Jimmy Shady's?

A remote dangled from the key ring. Zac hit the button. He heard the sound of a vehicle door unlocking. But Zac couldn't see which car was unlocking its door and flashing its lights.

Zac tried the remote over and over. But not one of the cars seemed to be opening.

Zac looked around him in frustration.

It was then that he saw it. There was a helipad on the roof of the town hall. With a brand-new, ultra-light stealth helicopter parked and waiting.

Zac tried the remote once again.

The helicopter's lights came on!

The doors opened!

He'd found his ride home.

As Zac ran towards the helipad, a brief doubt flickered through his mind. He'd never actually flown a helicopter before. Then again, in the past 24 hours, he'd piloted a fighter jet, won a gaming competition, raced around on a hover scooter, sung karaoke, and busted Jimmy Shady.

I bet I can handle a helicopter, thought Zac to himself.

···**THE END**···